I0788106

TOFFEE
APPLES

Poems and
Illustrations by

Isabel Bee

FOR MY FAMILY

Tried

I tried to make a Butterfly

I made the body first

Sculpting a clay abdomen

Antennae next ~ wire stuck in head.

Next I took the delicate paper,

Thin enough to see right through

I held it up in front of me

And throughout it I could see you.

I very carefully drew a line

Cut two pieces at a time

Each side to match the other,

The edges were all scalloped

~ This Butterfly would be like no other.

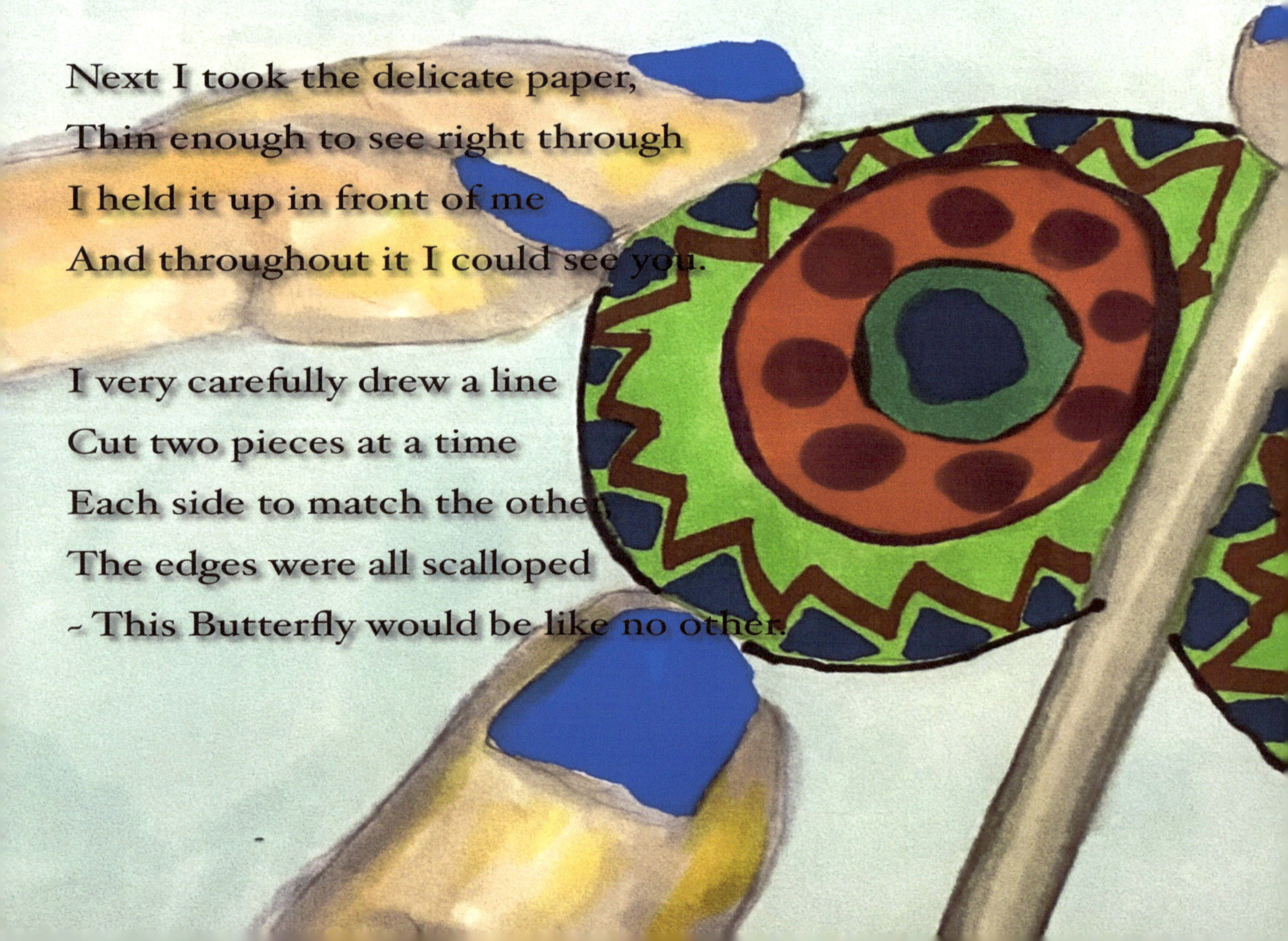

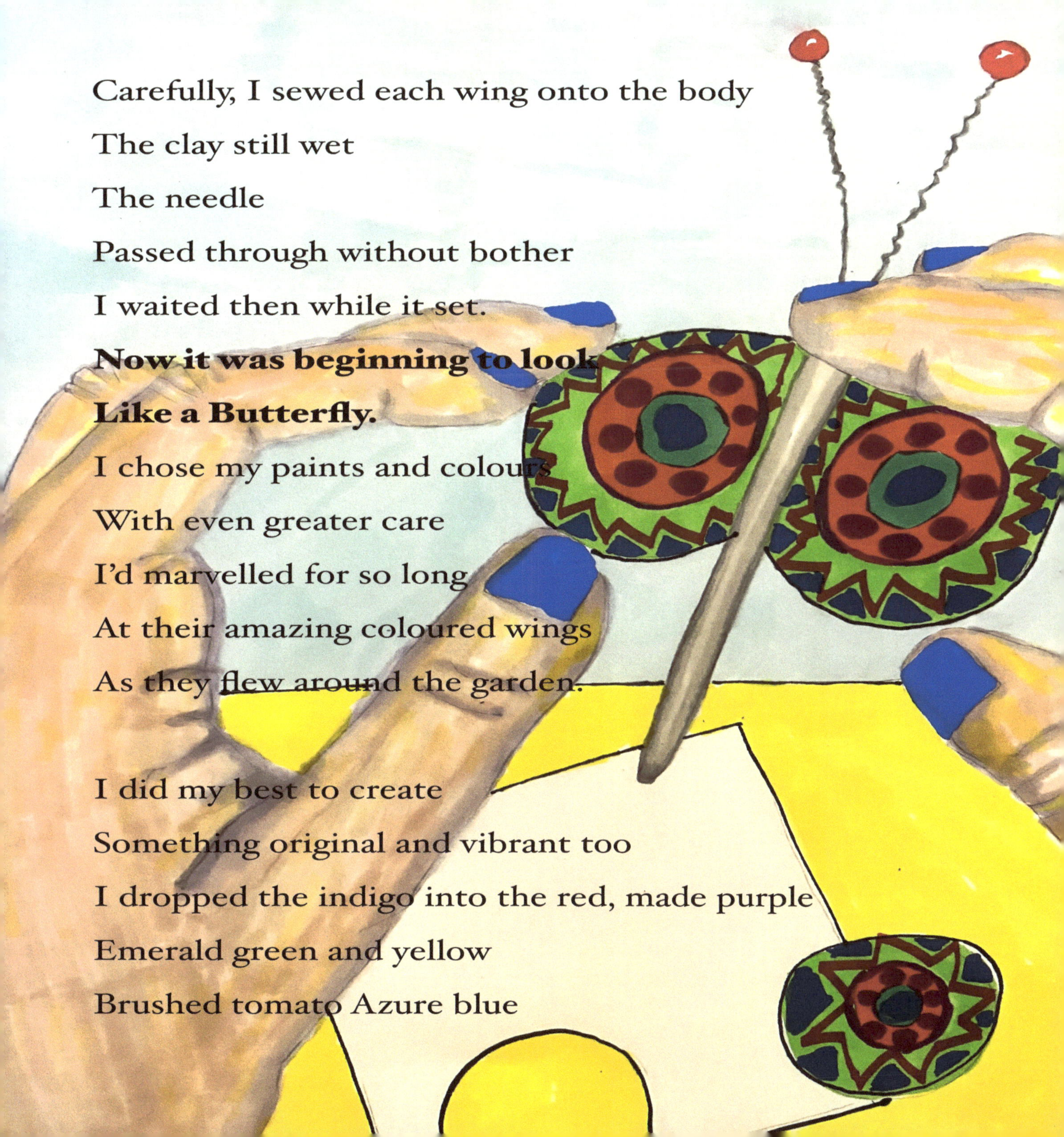

Carefully, I sewed each wing onto the body

The clay still wet

The needle

Passed through without bother

I waited then while it set.

Now it was beginning to look

Like a Butterfly.

I chose my paints and colours

With even greater care

I'd marvelled for so long

At their amazing coloured wings

As they flew around the garden.

I did my best to create

Something original and vibrant too

I dropped the indigo into the red, made purple

Emerald green and yellow

Brushed tomato Azure blue

Later on

Later on

I went to see my Butterfly,

I carefully touched its wings

I felt that they were dry.

I called out to my family

To come and see what I had made.

They came running excitedly

To come and see

I held the Butterfly high

High up above our heads

So it might look like it could fly.

It could have been enough

To see their smiling faces

Yet as I held it to the sky

I felt dismay that I could do no more

Than pretend to make it fly.

What sets the wings in motion?
Is where the marvel really lies.
What pulls it from its Chrysalis
And sends it up
Into the sky?

When The Rain Fell

When the rain fell
We lifted our faces
As some do to the sun

We watched
As others ran for cover
Popped up prepared
umbrellas.

Some looked on
Like we might be crazy

Drop by drop
Our hair-stuck in tendrils
To our now fresh faces

The days of longing for cleansing
Had come
We allowed in the newness
We allowed in the newness.

In the distance
The birds still sang
Songs of contented joy
In their feathered nests
And the Church bells rang.

WHAT IF

What if, but what if
Today was the day
We saw all our problems
From far far away?
The hot air balloon
That was promised so long
Arrived in our garden
Like the dream forgot so long.

It's glorious satin of stripes red and gold
That billowed as flames filled it full of hot
Air in the cold
We jumped in the basket
Thick ropes did untie
Up up and away
We drifted
To the sky.

Weightless was the air around us
Brighter was the sun
Happy was our laughter
As the life below
Was done.

We looked back then
On things we thought important~
To cut the grass, to trim the tree,
We saw now what really mattered
It was you
And it was me.

The sink we saw so tiny
Until it disappeared
Full of pots and spoons and cups
Where we often stood and argued
About the washing up.

The sheets they needed changing
That would not matter, not a jot
The laundry needed folding
We laughed
It was just a dot!

The Town where we would be so serious
About what we did and thought and said
Now was a tiny toy town
Like in the books
Our Mothers once read

The house in which we

Lived our lives

We once thought made us

Who we are

Faded under bright white clouds

Now we had the stars.

They glistened all around us

As the light it dimmed

Velvet azure enfolded us

In our warm and

Bright balloon

"NO MORE WASHING UP"

We cried

As we floated past

The moon.

FALL

They fall at last
Clinging must end softly
In silence. Unnoticed.
Except for when they are no more,
The branches bare again.

They land softly, without fuss.
Joining others
Together they wait.

There is something - a power
It reaches up
Pulls them under
Turns them over into the darkness, the dampness,
The Underground.

Beyond sun,
Time,
Laughter
Hate,
Disease
Beyond life
In all its forms

Broken down
They merge-
Feed roots
Grow up again
Life is transformed
It is Summer
Again.

THE LOW

The low light beckons
Paths covered in snow
Trees glisten on the bank below
Which way is it?
Which way will I go?

Dusk descends
Like pink velvet
Tree shadows draw lines
Like broomsticks
Still a path I have not picked.

Snow compacts
Beneath our feet
Footprints covered
-Life is fleeting
We press on
Lambs out of season.

Soon the blackened night arrives
Snow still guides
Our wearied eyes
Still it lights the path
So in the dark
In the dark,
We make our choice,
We make our mark.

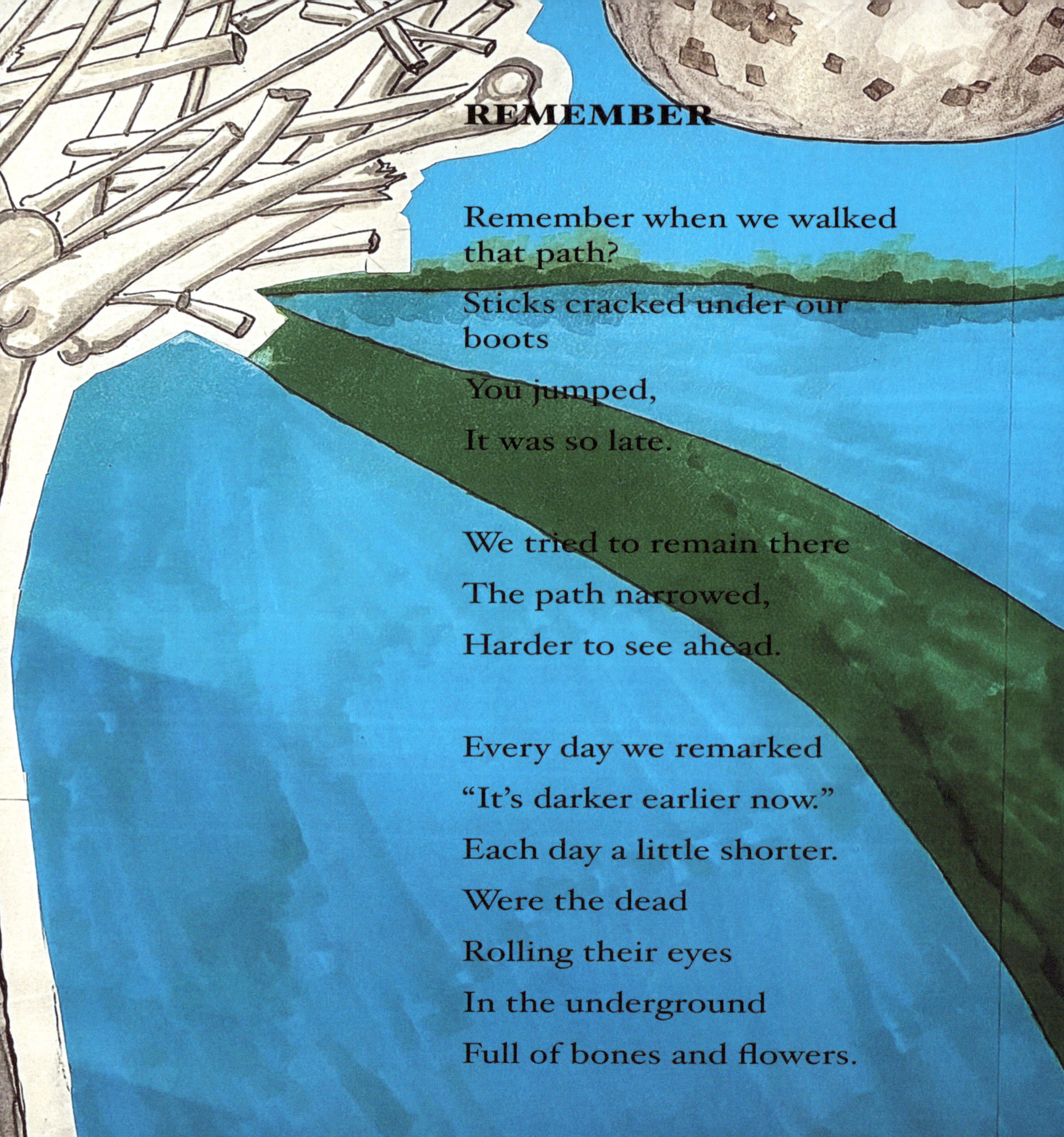

REMEMBER

Remember when we walked
that path?

Sticks cracked under our
boots

You jumped,

It was so late.

We tried to remain there

The path narrowed,

Harder to see ahead.

Every day we remarked

"It's darker earlier now."

Each day a little shorter.

Were the dead

Rolling their eyes

In the underground

Full of bones and flowers.

Day by day our shadows lengthened
Once sweet birdsong, now sound bites
Darkness falls around us
Trees bare bones
Stood Trembling

Trees bare bones
Stood trembling.

Now is the time of watching, waiting.
We walk on with stooped backs
Guided by the only light that remained
That in each others hearts
We walked onwards
Into the dark.

RISE

Our white bed sheets
Floated outside our windows
Thousands of backward parachutes
The morning Sun poured
Into the darkness.

Not a typical thing
To happen mid October
The clouds parted
Graciously.

Our frightened houses
Sensing the change
Cling to the earth
-Built for saftey, not flying.

We the people
Watch them rising
Beyond all human understanding
So sing now for the first time
In a thousand years.

TO

Man Alive

I'm sure there is no man alive
That does't sit and wonder ~~
Doesn't have a song
Who doesn't heave a heavy sigh
Once the day
Is done.
But does he ever wonder
Just what it is that's wrong?

Or does he look for myriad ways
To escape the toll?
The tunnel is there
It does not move
Someday, must be driven through.

He could maybe take the scenic route

Gaze at the endless winding road,

It maybe would take longer

But the scenery will be good.

Perhaps he'll take a different road-

One without the tunnel

It doesn't go where he'd like to go

But he will avoid the toll that way

And does the destination really matter?

Maybe he'll decide, once and for all,

The road's not really for him at all

He may decide to fly

Not use the road at all.

The turbulence was great

As he flew towards the sun,

The drugs they did their job

Yet were not so great

Once all was said, and done.

There was once a man from way back

Who walked right through the tunnel

He paid the price

While people mocked

"Should have gone by car," they said

He carried on regardless

Reached just where he needed to

He didn't take a map

Now he is a happy man

And never does look back.

Only once

Only once

He turned around to see

So many men in misery

Pretending they were free.

TOL

Wondered

I wondered to the garden,
I had not been there so long'
I could see my breathing
The path seemed longer
Than it was in Summer.

The leaves have almost fallen,
They cover everything,
A cosy blanket - warm, I hope
To protect the living things,
Until the time
Until the time
When they are called
To rise again.

I Woke

I woke

I woke up

Into the day

And everything around me

Around me shouted to say

"HURRY, HURRY, JOIN THE RACE."

The man in his car

The woman on woman's hour

The trucks rushing by

The woman on her scooter

Delivering pizza

Shoppers with bags

Breaking their backs

Full of the latest designer crap

Politicians working on saving themselves

The war mongers

Hoping to win the world

The hard Estate Agent

Selling the dream.

TERMS OF YOUR EMPLOYMENT
ZERO HOURS
NO SICK PAY
NO HOLIDAY PAY
MINIMUM WAGE
BLAH BLAH BLAH
Radio
DIGITAL
Bro, be in your area- Bangin' gear- text me
Safe Sound PIZZA
DEATH TOLL NOW 30,000 PEOPLE
DESIGNER
ESTATE

The prisoner

The victims

The carers

The dying

Time is running out

Something no-one is buying….

And….**STOP!!!!!!!!!**

I woke I woke

Into the day

I glanced in the mirror

Put hand on heart

And the is what

I heard it say,

"Show me, PLEASE,

Show me some love today"

High Tide

So what to do?

Resist? Hide? Live? Die?

As the Autumn chill creeps

Through now grey skies

I'm warming my foot

On the radiator beside my bed.

There are wrinkles where my ankle twists

I've done so much now

All from here

With my trusty 'phone

Many times over

I saved your life.

I thought of Jesus

And His melancholy madness

"Look at Me then you can walk on water."   (Cont'd..)

It was tempting~

To walk that bright path towards the sun.

If we looked hard enough,

Would we make it?

And I am pondering

Just how strange and unusual

That a silvery fish-

About a foot long

Would leap from the sea

Just in front of where we sat

And land with a giant splash

And if it is worth trying

To figure out

What it all might mean.

How Is It

How is it

You still have not found

What you're looking for?

You who looked into the bright lights

Performed and were adored

You dined in Palaces

Gold gilt rooms,

Laughed with Princes.

When I was a child

It wasn't sunlit beaches

Attractions, poolside that my heart

Belonged to.

There were craggy rocks I once climbed

In windy sunshine-

My element.

But mostly

My heart belongs to the farm

Where absolute silence

What is the dearest sound

And straw and hay and animals

We are breathing steam

And I could see

1 million stars.

And now I know

Where to find the Baby

With his Mother

Her warm breath

Covering his tiny body

He is gentle smile

Saving the world.

Toffee Apple

The road seemed long
To tiny legs
Hand in hand
We made it to the funfair
Won a goldfish
I loved how the Hall of Mirrors
Made my head tall.

Wurlitzer spins
Disorientated
My stretched out head
You gave me that toffee apple
Didn't you.

So sweet coated caramel
Milk teeth
Cracked it open
I looked inside
The core was black.

You gave me the toffee apple
Didn't you

Me with my stretched out head
Still spinning
You chose your moments
Told me nothing was real.

Me.
Me and my fertile imagination.

with the
iple who had ack omb f lso went
Till thi mo t they ha d to unde d the
at he the dead.
nday o

Forever

Forever and for all eternity

Are things we try to see

Yet forever and eternity

Are so hard to believe.

Especially, when you or just you

And I am just me.

We gaze into the night sky,

See stars twinkling so magically

Forever and for all eternity

Are things we try to see

Yet forever and eternity

Are so hard to believe.

Especially, when you or just you

And I am just me.

Photograph from Authors Page to Stage Interactive performance workshop

immersive event performance   'The Song of the Butterfly' adapted for stage

From The Butterfly Who Wouldn't Open Her Wings 2020

We look out across the ocean

As the waves look at our feet

The water comes out spirit

As we try to see eternity

But there is always a horizon

And you are you,

And I am me.

We close our eyes tight shirt

And imagine a blissful seen

Maybe a woodland full of bluebells

Who are gentle running stream

But all imaginings end.

And still you are just you,

And I am just me.

So we gaze at one another,

And in the others eyes we see,

All the twinkling stars,

The oceans

And the streams.

At last

We see that in each other,

Lies forever,

And eternity.

We very much hope you loved this book of poems and illustrations by Isabel Bee.

Isabel holds an MFA from Middlesex University in the UK and is the Author and Illustrator of The Butterfly Who Wouldn't Open Her Wings 2020, The Plum Tree 2021, Fox and Dog 2021 and Flesh 2022. Isabel has also adapted her book The Butterfly Who Wouldn't Open Her Wings for the Stage (Song of the Butterfly) It has been performed five times in various venues with press articles available.

www.ingramcontent.com/pod-product-compliance
Lightning Source LLC
Chambersburg PA
CBHW041419300726
48981CB00007B/343